Cape Cod Bear

ISBN: 1478360372
ISBN 13: 9781478360377
Library of Congress Control Number: 2012914223
CreateSpace Independent Publishing Platform
North Charleston, South Carolina

Cape Cod Bear

Written by Kathleen Ready Dayan
Illustrated by Kate Walls

Barney, a young black bear, lived deep in the woods with his mother. But he knew that soon he would have his own family. His mom had told him so.

One spring night while out exploring he stopped for a drink of water and a mischievous raccoon dared him to swim across the river.

Bears are good swimmers, but this river was too strong. It swept Barney away from his home in the woods to a place no bear had ever been.

He walked for days looking for tree markings made by other bears, but he found none. All the animals he met told him they had never seen a black bear.

"You are lost," said the fish in Plymouth Harbor.

Barney didn't want to be a lost bear.

In the harbor was a replica of the ship that had brought the pilgrims to America. Barney felt like they must have felt, lonely and scared of his new surroundings.

The next night he entered a neighborhood and noticed a sign with human markings on it. Did the sign mean *Wildlife Welcome* or *No Bears Allowed?*

It was only May so there were no berries yet to eat, but he found crackers under a swing set and half a banana near a trash can. He was eating seed from a birdfeeder when the homeowner turned on a light. Barney scampered up a tree.

Word spread quickly--a bear was in the neighborhood!

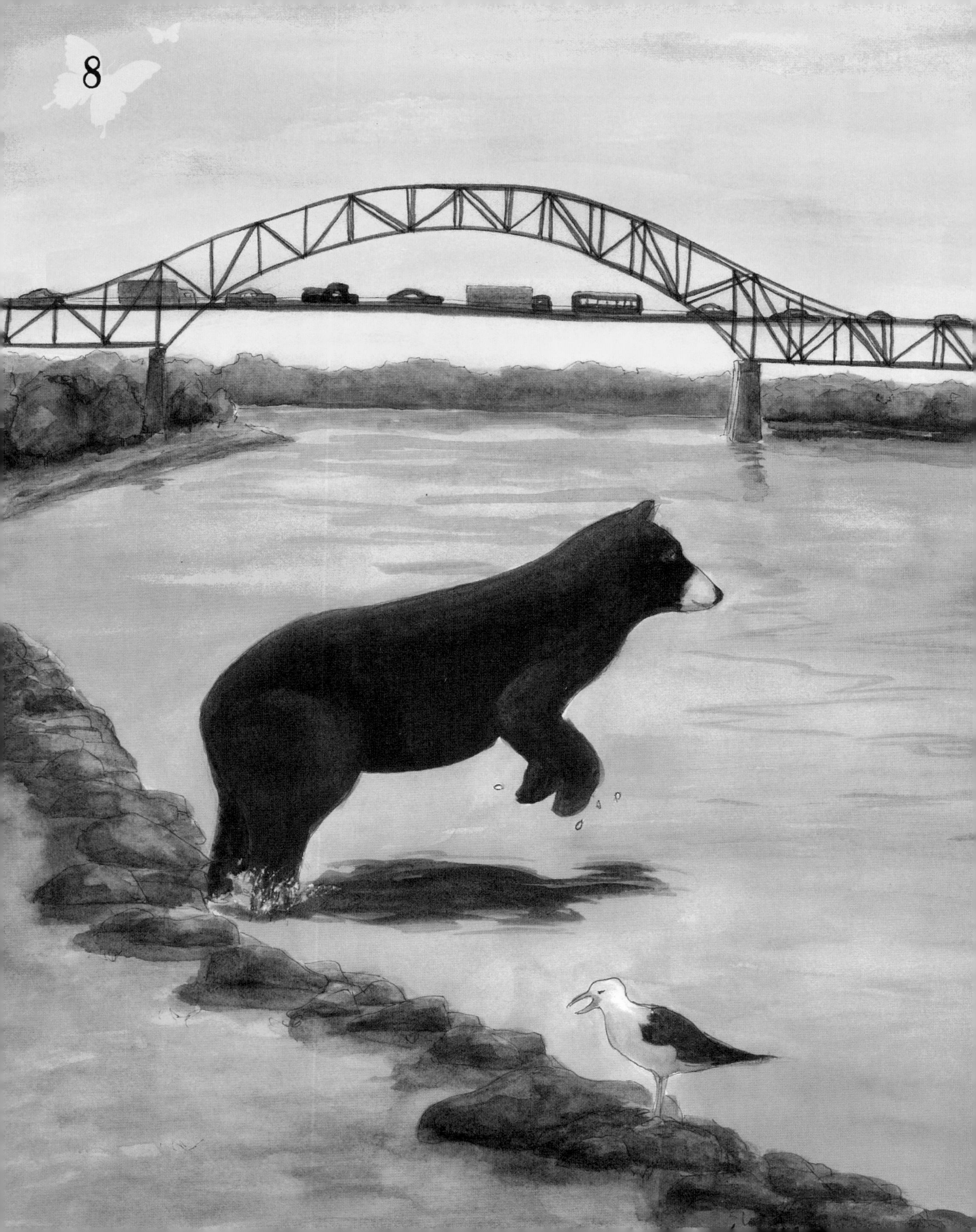

Once the curious people went to bed, Barney climbed down the tree. He walked all night until he reached the Cape Cod Canal. There was a traffic jam on the Sagamore Bridge that stretched across it.

"Where is everyone going?" he asked the large white birds flying over him.

"To Cape Cod!" the birds sang out like a chorus. "Everyone vacations there!"

Barney wanted to have a Cape Cod vacation, too, like the humans and the white birds with loud voices. He dove into the canal, swam across...

...and he was on Cape Cod!

Early the next morning he followed a path to the Sandwich Boardwalk. There were markings on the wooden planks under his paws. When bears left markings it was to send messages to other bears, for instance to let them know it was a good place to find food.

That was it! Right underneath him fish were swimming. How nice of the humans to let him know! Barney leaped off the boardwalk into the seawater.

The next day he entered the Long Pasture Wildlife Sanctuary in Barnstable and liked it so much that he spent many days there.

He swam in the cold marsh water, ate salty fish, and watched the humans go by in their little boats.

Although he never knew it, that was how he acquired his human name—Barney—because he lingered so long in Barnstable.

It was dawn when Barney arrived at Taylor-Bray Farm in Yarmouth Port and right away noticed two unusual animals watching him.

They were Fiona and Scotty, Scottish Highland cows. They'd never seen a bear. "A-ooh! A-ooh! A-ooh!" they bellowed.

Barney stood on his back legs so they could see how big he was. But they were bigger than him! The ground shook beneath his feet as they galloped toward him.

Barney ran. He ran over the town line, through a wooded area and into Dennis. He ran until he suddenly stopped short in front of the Cape Cod Museum of Art...

...and nearly landed in a very small pond. It had a lovely fairy house in it. Barney peered into the pool and to his delight saw another bear. Another bear!

Cautiously he edged his muzzle toward it. Barney's nose touched the cold water and he realized the bear was only his reflection. He was still alone.

The next night he crossed into Brewster where he peeked in the windows of the Cape Cod Museum of Natural History and saw the motionless birds and fish swimming in glass cases.

What a vacation he was having!

In Drummer Boy Park he slept next to the Old Higgins Farm Windmill. When he awakened he found the Stony Brook Herring Run where he caught his breakfast.

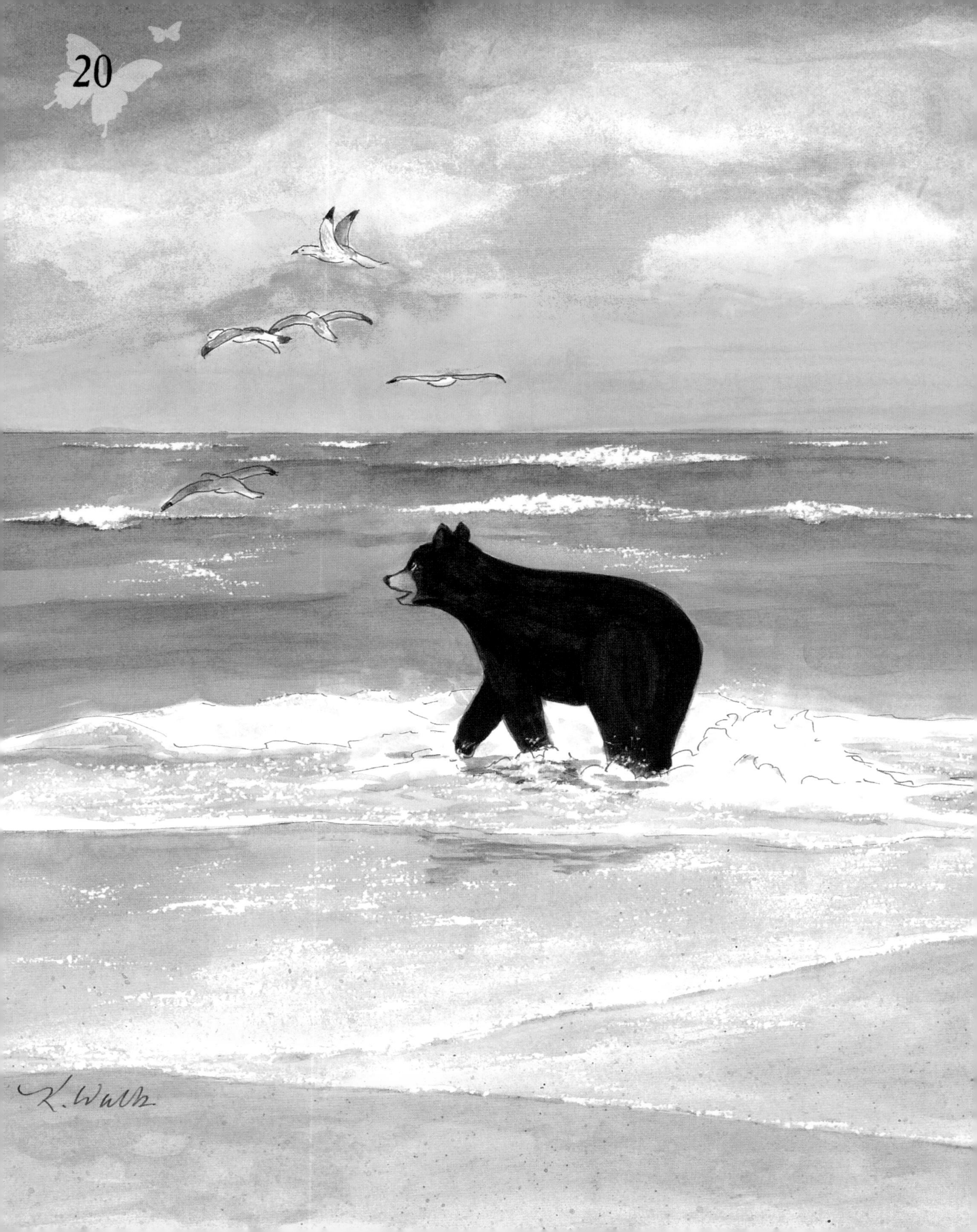

He arrived in Orleans late at night and found his way to Priscilla Landing at the Cape Cod National Seashore.

At sunrise, he watched the sky turn colors on Nauset Beach. Then Barney waded in the waves with the sea birds. He tried to catch them, but they were much too fast!

That night he saw the Nauset Light shining like a star high on a cliff and walked in its direction onto Nauset Light Beach in Eastham.

On Marconi Beach in Wellfleet, Barney spotted a dog with his human. He made a clacking sound with his teeth to scare him off. But the dog was very brave.

He chased Barney all the way to the top of a very tall staircase, through some trees and across the highway! Finally the chase ended and Barney found himself at the Truro Vineyards of Cape Cod.

There were many rows of plants, but it was too early in the season for the fruit to be ripe. Barney made a meal of grape leaves instead.

He was sound asleep in the sand dunes of Provincetown when one of the loud white birds awakened him. Barney followed it to MacMillan Pier where the biggest creature he'd ever seen was blowing mist out of the top of its head!

"How surprising to meet a little black bear in Provincetown," the whale said.

"I'm not so very little," Barney replied. "My mom says I'll find a mate soon."

"Go home little bear," the whale advised. "You won't find a mate on Cape Cod."

Barney was lonely for the company of other bears so he took the whale's advice. He began the trek back, following his own paw prints and tree markings.

Cars zoomed past him at frightening speeds. He wished he could tell the humans: "Slow down, look around. Feel the grass with your paws and taste the salty sea."

Near Gull Pond in Wellfleet he was homesick as he fell asleep in a tree.

When he awakened Barney was deep in the woods of Western Massachusetts. And right away he knew that he was home.

The Cape Cod Bear, that later came to be known as "Barney", was first spotted in Middleboro in May of 2012 and was next seen in the Ponds of Plymouth neighborhood in Plymouth. Shortly thereafter sightings were reported all the way down Route 6A on Cape Cod to the point at Provincetown. He was ultimately tranquilized on June 11, 2012 in Wellfleet and was set free in the woods of Western Massachusetts. Later the same month he was found and tranquilized once again in Brookline before being returned to the woods a second time. What was once a lost bear is now a famous bear. Everyone on Cape Cod knows of Barney. He even has his own Facebook page, Twitter account and website!

You can find Barney at www.capecodbearbook.com. Visit us on Facebook: Cape Cod Bear Book.

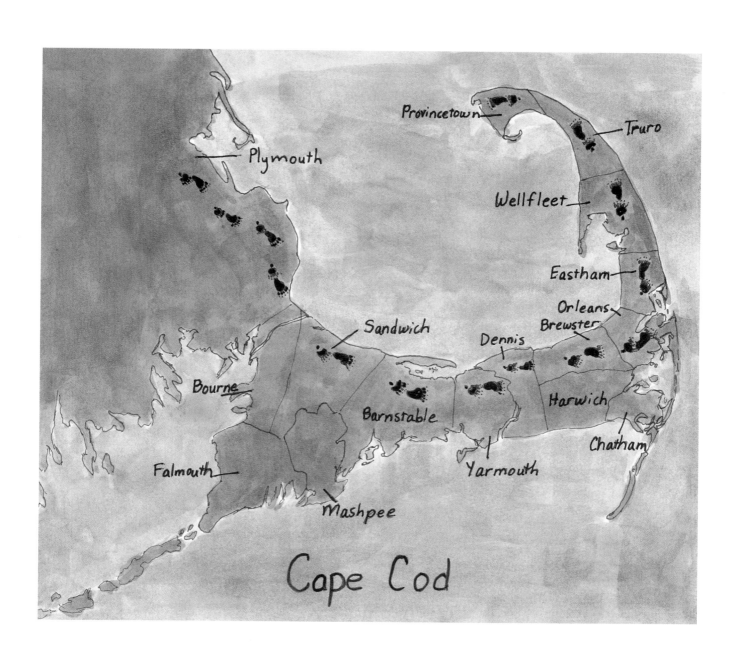

Cape Cod

20028441R00019

Made in the USA
Charleston, SC
23 June 2013